THIS SERIES OF BOOKS
IS DEDICATED TO THE MEMORY OF
ANNE-MARIE DALMAIS
WHOSE GREAT ENTHUSIASM
AND INSPIRATION MADE THIS
PROJECT COME TO LIFE

Four Little Friends

GYO FUJIKAWA

HAVE FUN
TOGETHER
and other tales

Modern Publishing
A Division of Unisystems, Inc.
New York, New York 10022
Printed in Italy

HAVE FUN TOGETHER

Four little friends
Out to have some fun,
They're picking juicy berries
And tasting every one.

Rags sits patiently,
Hoping his wait will end,
And Sam will find some berries
To share with his best friend.

Next they reach the stream:
They want to take a swim.
Everyone has fun, 'cept Sam,
Who slips and falls right in!

When the day is over,
The four friends slowly roam
Across the fields and meadows
As they head for home.

FOLLOW THE LEADER

Brian led the friends
As they played their favorite game.
When he walked, or climbed, or jumped,
They had to do the same.

"Follow the leader," Brian shouted
To the friends he led.
Next it would be Patsy's turn
To take the lead instead.

One by one each little friend
Got to take the lead.
Taking turns is the best way
To make friendship succeed.

GOOD DOG, RAGS

Sam's kitten wore a bonnet
That got tangled in a hedge.
The four friends tried to free her
From where she was wedged.

The kitten was afraid.
No one knew just what to do.
Until Sam's brave dog, Rags,
Came to the rescue!

QUIET TIME

There are many times to play with friends,
To jump and shout and run.
But sometimes being by yourself
Can be just as much fun.

ABC TEA PARTY

A, B, C
Come to Patsy's tea party!

D, E, F
She invited lots of guests.

G, H, I
There will be cookies and pie.

J, K, L
Lots of secrets to tell

M, N, O
Dress in ribbons and bows.

P, Q, R
It isn't very far.

S, T, U
You're invited too.

V, W, X, Y, Z
We'll meet under the tree!

FOREVER FRIENDS

Fast, faster, fastest, the friends ran down the hill.
Brian was in the lead until he took a spill.

High, higher, highest, the friends jumped toward the sky.
They tried to touch the clouds as they floated by.

Big, bigger, biggest, the friends climbed up the trees.
The cool air touched their faces; they smiled in the breeze.

Loud, louder, loudest, the friends laughed and played all day,
Enjoying the summer sun and its warming rays.

Slow, slower, slowest, the friends sat down to rest.
Sharing time together is what the friends do best.